HOW TO BE A BOSS

WITHDRAWN

3/17

HOW TO BE A
BOSS

adapted by Tina Gallo
illustrated by Elsa Chang

Ready-to-Read

Simon Spotlight

New York   London   Toronto   Sydney   New Delhi

SIMON SPOTLIGHT
An imprint of Simon & Schuster Children's Publishing Division
1230 Avenue of the Americas, New York, New York 10020
This Simon Spotlight edition February 2017
The Boss Baby © 2017 DreamWorks Animation LLC. All Rights Reserved.
All rights reserved, including the right of reproduction in whole or in part in any form.
SIMON SPOTLIGHT, READY-TO-READ, and colophon are registered
trademarks of Simon & Schuster, Inc.
For information about special discounts for bulk purchases, please contact
Simon & Schuster Special Sales at 1-866-506-1949 or business@simonandschuster.com.
Manufactured in the United States of America 0117 LAK
2 4 6 8 10 9 7 5 3 1
ISBN 978-1-4814-7009-4 (hc)
ISBN 978-1-4814-7008-7 (pbk)
ISBN 978-1-4814-7010-0 (eBook)

Hello, and welcome!
Thank you for joining me today.
My name is Boss Baby, but you
can call me BB.

You are here to take my class,
How to Be a Boss.

Do you have what it takes?
We shall see!

Lesson one:
You are in charge.

Let your voice be heard!

Lesson two:
Demand twenty-four-hour room service!

Remember to do what you want,
all the time!

Lesson three:
Claim the center
of the room.
You need to keep an eye
on everything and everyone.

Lesson four:
Always keep people
around to do your work
for you.

Some might call this
a playdate,
but it is a work date!

Lesson five:
You are the boss.
You hand out the rewards.

Lesson six: Being a boss is tiring.

Power nap whenever you can.

Lesson seven:
Everyone thinks babies
are adorable.

Use this to your advantage!

Lesson eight:
Many important deals
are made over drinks.

Always have beverages
at your meetings!

Lesson nine:
Relax when you can.

Demand a private gym
and spa!
You deserve it!

Lesson ten:
Sometimes you will be asked
to wear silly outfits.

Resist this whenever
possible!

Sometimes, however,
it will pay to look silly.

Choose your battles wisely!

Lesson eleven:
Your family has one job—
to keep you happy!

Lesson twelve:
This is the most important
lesson: Show your family
you love them.
But just a little bit.

And not all the time.
Always leave them
wanting more!

Congratulations!
You are now a boss baby!
Now you have to go
because I need to go.
Go potty, that is! Good-bye!